GH☺STBUSTERS™

WHO YOU GONNA CALL?

Adapted by John Sazaklis • Illustrated by Alan Batson

Based on the Screenplay Written by Katie Dippold & Paul Feig
Based on the 1984 film "Ghostbusters" An Ivan Reitman Film
Written by Dan Aykroyd and Harold Ramis
Directed by Paul Feig

🦅 A GOLDEN BOOK • NEW YORK

Ghostbusters TM & © 2016 Columbia Pictures Industries, Inc. All Rights Reserved. Published in the United States
by Golden Books, an imprint of Random House Children's Books, a division of Penguin Random House LLC,
1745 Broadway, New York, NY 10019, and in Canada by Penguin Random House Canada Limited, Toronto.
Golden Books, A Golden Book, A Little Golden Book, the G colophon, and the distinctive gold spine
are registered trademarks of Penguin Random House LLC.
randomhousekids.com
Educators and librarians, for a variety of teaching tools, visit us at RHTeachersLibrarians.com
ISBN 978-1-5247-1491-8 (trade) — ISBN 978-1-5247-1492-5 (ebook)
Printed in the United States of America
10 9 8 7 6 5 4 3 2 1

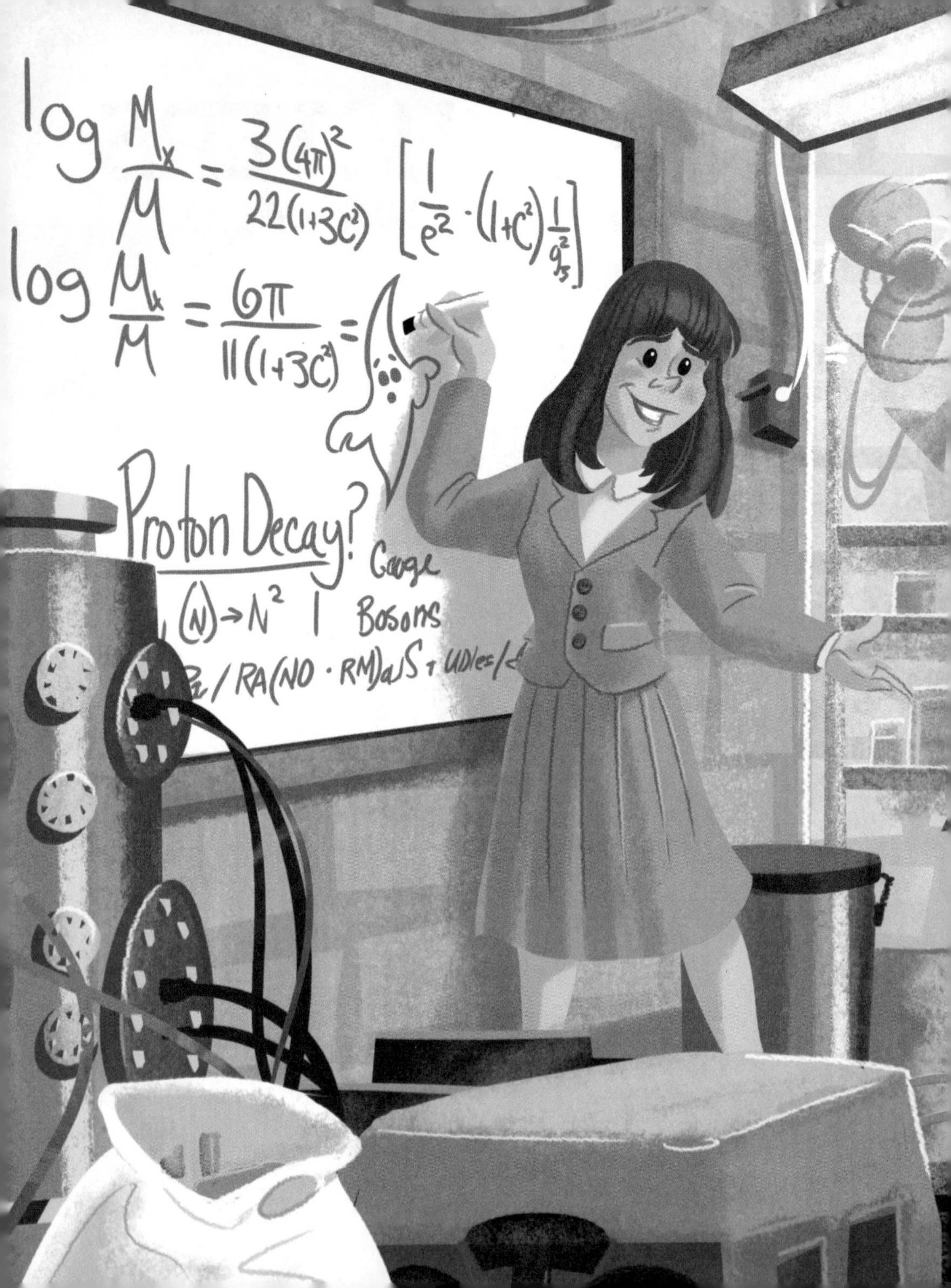
Proton Decay?
Gauge
Bosons

Erin Gilbert, **Abby Yates**, and **Jillian Holtzmann** were scientists in New York City who studied ghosts. They believed ghosts were real, but they didn't have any proof. They were determined to change that by making contact with the spirit world.

Erin had heard that the old Aldridge mansion was haunted, so she got the team together to investigate. Inside they found a **REAL GHOST**, and it *wasn't* scary at all! In fact, the ghostly lady was eerily beautiful.

Erin approached it and said, "She looks so peaceful!"

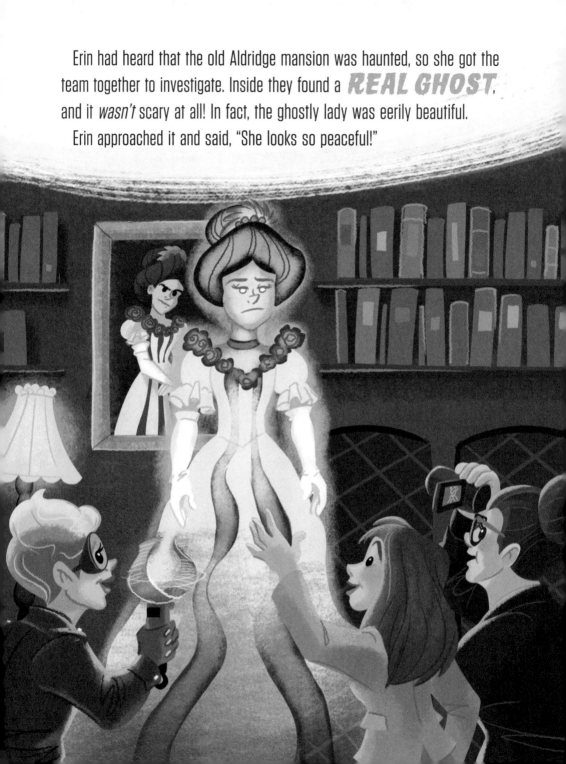

But in a flash, the ghost turned nasty and sprayed slime all over her.

Abby was thrilled. "Ghosts *are* real!" she said. "That means they could be all over New York!"

With more and more ghosts beginning to haunt the city, Erin, Abby, and Holtzmann became **GHOSTBUSTERS**. Even though their office was above an old Chinese restaurant, and their receptionist, Kevin, wasn't very helpful, *and* they didn't have a car, the team was ready to start ghost hunting.

Holtzmann got busy. She went to work creating **proton packs** and **traps**. "If we're gonna catch ghosts," she said, "we're gonna need a lot of juice!"

The next day, **Patty Tolan**, a subway employee, followed a man named **Rowan** into a train tunnel. He was doing something suspicious with a strange device that started to spark and glow.

A frightening ghost named **SPARKY** appeared, scaring Patty out of her wits! But she knew who she could call for help.

After meeting the Ghostbusters, Patty joined the team. She had read books about New York and knew the city better than anyone. Patty borrowed uniforms for the team from her subway job, and she even got them a car. They named it **Ecto-1**.

Now they were officially ready for business. First stop: a supernatural disturbance at a heavy-metal concert.

The Ghostbusters arrived at the concert hall, where a menacing ghost named **MAYHEM** had trashed the stage. Erin shouted, "Let's crash this paranormal party!"

The team used their proton beams to hold Mayhem while Holtzmann threw down her trap to catch the monstrous ghost.

The crowd went wild! They thought it was part of the show.

Backstage at the concert, the Ghostbusters found another device like the one Patty had seen in the subway tunnel. Rowan was there, too! When he ran off, the Ghostbusters followed him to the Mercado Hotel, where he worked as a janitor.

"What are you up to?" Abby asked, tracking him down to his workshop in the hotel's basement.

"My machines have finally broken the barrier between the spirit world and ours!" he cackled as he unleashed a horde of horrible ghosts!

The ghosts from Rowan's portal poured into the streets. The Ghostbusters followed them and found themselves in the middle of an eerie Thanksgiving Day parade with giant balloon ghosts!

Rowan's machine turned him into a ghostly ghoul, too!
He ordered his marching mob to attack the Ghostbusters.
"That's a lot of creepy!" Patty exclaimed.

Holtzmann launched a proton grenade that blew the nearest nasties into puddles of ectoplasmic ghost goo.

The Ghostbusters fired up their proton packs and fought their way through the ghosts.

CRACKLE!

POP!

Rowan was furious. He transformed himself into a giant ghost and tried to stomp the Ghostbusters!

The team made a narrow escape.

"We need to close that portal!" Abby cried. The Ghostbusters combined their proton power into one concentrated stream of energy aimed at the portal.

There was a mighty explosion, and then the portal began to pull the spirits back into their own dimension.

Unable to escape its pull, Rowan vanished into the swirling portal, too!

The Ghostbusters had single-handedly saved the city
from paranormal peril.
Now everyone in New York knew exactly who to call!